# Chasing Time

*Eager to redress a year-old mistake, Hunter constructs a machine to transcend temporal limitations. But he only creates an insurmountable paradox.*

After more than three decades, storyteller and poet F.I. Goldhaber continues writing professionally. As a reporter, editor, business writer, and marketing communications consultant, she produced words for newspapers, corporations, governments, and non-profits in five states.

She wins awards for her fiction and poetry. Preditors & Editors readers poll ranked her second poetry collection, *Pairs of Poems,* third internationally. Various organizations honor her erotica works. Her short stories, novelettes, poems, news stories, feature articles, essays, editorial columns, and reviews appear in magazines, ezines, newspapers, calendars, and anthologies. She also published five erotica novels under another name.

In addition to paper, electronic, and audio publications, F.I. shares her words at events in Salem, Keizer, Portland, Seattle and on the radio. She appeared at venues such as Wordstock, Oregon Literary Review, bookstores, libraries, and Chemeketa Community College; gives presentations on subjects as diverse as marketing, writing erotica, and building volunteer organizations; and taught Introduction to Indie Publishing at Portland Community College and as a weekend intensive.

**http://goldhaber.net/**

# Chasing Time

Even if we travel to the past, can we atone for prior mistakes?

# F.I. Goldhaber

*Chasing Time*

Fantastic Worlds Publishing

ISBN:   978-1-937839-18-5

Copyright © 2014 by F.I. Goldhaber

Fantastic Worlds Publishing
http://fantasticworldspublishing.com
P.O. Box 80766
Portland OR 97280

# Acknowledgements

Many thanks to all those I have learned from through the years, especially the Wordos professional writers workshop and Larry Brooks. Thanks also to those who have freely shared their knowledge online notably Dean Wesley Smith and Kristine Kathryn Rusch. Those who inspired me to pursue writing from an early age include Ruth Wright my fifth and sixth grade teacher at Randolph Elementary School in Huntsville, Alabama, Nancy Travis my freshman English teacher at Clear Creek High School in Texas, and most prominently my parents, Jerry and Bev Goldhaber. Very special thanks to my editor, Laurie Lawhon of Fine Tune Your Words, Jay Lake and Dr. Steven Goldhaber for their assistance with this story, and my beloved husband Joel Goldhaber.

# Chasing Time

## By F.I. Goldhaber

**H**unter glanced at the clock, dismayed when he realized he had spent the past six hours buffing the housing of one marine lamp. He cursed the unusual dearth of quality artifacts at scrap yards in the area. Although he should have left for the convention center twenty minutes ago, he needed to spiff up first before he headed downtown. Abandoning the components scattered across the top of his primary workbench — a door harvested from a thrift shop dumpster then sheathed in sheet steel — he headed upstairs.

By the time Hunter showered, trimmed his mostly black goatee, combed his thinning black hair, removed the brass polish from under his fingernails, and put on clean clothing, he knew he would not make the lecture of the American he had "met" on a dating site. He arrived at the conference center just as Dr. Melinda Jacobson received an enthusiastic round of applause from the audience of about seventy-five. Hunter waited until the last autograph seeker finally left before approaching the beautiful brunette, who sat behind stacks of books at a table next to the podium.

"Good evening, Miss. I'm Hunter Davidson." She looked up, but he saw no recognition in her dark brown, almost black eyes. "Umm, we corresponded a while back about hooking up, but with you in Pennsylvania and me here in Toronto, well, I was never able to get down to the States to meet you."

Her lips turned up, but the smile did not touch her eyes, which if anything seemed tinged with sadness. "I'm afraid that puts you in a group of a hundred or so men. And, I stopped participating in anything related to online dating more than a year ago, so you'll forgive me for not recognizing the name." She looked him up and down. "Did you wish to purchase a book or get an autograph?"

"No." He touched the stack of volumes covered with shiny gold dust jackets, amazed at how many people he had watched shell out thirty dollars Canadian for her advice on surviving a recession. "I was hoping since you've ventured north, we could do that laboratory analysis we missed out on last year." The picture she sent him when she invited him to visit her in Erie did not do her justice at all. Now, seeing her in person, he kicked himself for not making more of an effort then. Her long hair fell well past her shoulders and framed a delicate face, accenting creamy skin. She wore pink lipstick that made her lips stand out and ask to be kissed. The scoop neckline of her blue dress revealed a cleavage he wanted to bury his face in.

She raised one eyebrow. "Laboratory analysis?"

"Yes. To quote one of your e-mails, our 'minds were inexorably drawn to each other,' but we needed an in-person meeting to find out if there was any chemistry. I'm not sure which of us started referring to it as 'laboratory analysis.'"

She brought a suitcase up from under the table and removed sheets of bubble wrap from it. "If you're not interested in a book or an autograph, you'll have to excuse me, I need to get ready for this evening's reception."

"Sorry I didn't stay in touch, but I was hoping, since you've ventured up to Toronto, we could spend a little time together and see if there's any foundation for a relationship."

She shook her head and wrapped the remaining books. "Not looking anymore."

His shoulders sagged. When he had seen announcements for her only Canadian engagement, Hunter had read everything he could find about her online to determine if she'd gotten involved with someone else. But, he had seen nothing that mentioned any relationship. "You've found someone?"

"No. Just stopped looking." She stacked the wrapped books inside the suitcase.

"May I ask why?"

She looked up at him. Standing, she only came up to his chest even though he was barely six feet tall. "I decided I was better off putting the time and emotional energy I wasted looking for a relationship into my research." She zipped the half-empty suitcase closed. "At least there, I have something to show for it."

Before he could offer assistance, she lowered the case to the floor.

"May I help you with that?"

"No thanks." She pulled out the handle and tilted the suitcase forward onto its wheels. "I've got it."

"I don't suppose you'd allow me to buy you dinner?"

"Don't have time. Besides, I'm sure there'll be food at the reception." She pulled the suitcase across the conference room toward the exit.

"Please, Melinda." He hurried ahead so he could open the door for her. "I've regretted not meeting you for more than a year now. I'd really appreciate an opportunity to spend just an hour with you. Our e-mail correspondence very much intrigued me. If it wasn't for your country's xenophobic border patrol and my workload at the time, I'm sure I'd have made it down to visit you."

"Regardless, as I said, I'm no longer interested in forming a relationship. I've carefully structured my life around being single. I even sold my house in Erie and moved to a tiny condo in Philadelphia." She genuinely smiled for the first time since he had approached her table. "No room for anyone else."

He remembered that in one of their last email exchanges she had mentioned that she planned to sell her house because it was too big for one person. She had asked Hunter to accelerate his attempts to visit because selling it made less sense to her if they ended up together. But the prospect of moving his workshop to the States, when he was badly behind on getting out commissioned pieces, had been a big part of why he had stopped writing her.

"Surely, you must get lonely sometimes?" He walked along beside her through the corridor that connected the conference center with the hotel. Despite her height, she kept up a brisk pace.

She shrugged. "Not really. Research, teaching, promoting this book, and writing the next one, all keep me quite busy." She stopped in front of the hotel elevator. "Good evening."

"There must be something I can do to convince you to spend some time with me while you're in Toronto?"

She raised one eyebrow again, which made

her look both formidable and absolutely ador-
able. "Tell me, exactly how'd the correspondence between us end?"

He dropped his chin to his chest. "I'm afraid,
I stopped responding to your e-mails."

She tilted her head to one side. "You're that
maker guy, aren't you? The one who builds
fancy brass and wooden desktop catapults and
likes to pontificate about string theory."

"Yes." He smiled, hoping something had trig-
gered a positive memory, and looked up in time
to see her eyes turn stone cold. "Even if I had
any interest in getting involved with anyone,
which I don't, why ever would it be with someone that rude and inconsiderate?"

"Please accept my humblest apologies for my
rudeness, not — I assure you — intentional or
personal. At the time, I was just overwhelmed
by circumstances. I'd do just about anything if
you'd let me make it up to you."

"Guess you'll have to make a time machine
then, 'cause I completely lost interest when you
severed all communication without any kind of
explanation."

The elevator door opened with a ping and she
pulled the suitcase inside, turning and staring
at Hunter in a way that prevented him from
moving until the doors slid closed again.

He headed for his truck, running through
the parking lot trying to avoid getting drenched.
At the time they had first corresponded, Hunter had thought Melinda the dreamiest woman

he had ever exchanged e-mail with — until she sent him her photograph. Although it did not turn him off, it did not exactly inspire him to overcome all the border crossing complications, and she could not visit him until the end of the school term — long after he stopped writing. Now that he had met her, though, he decided she was the woman he had been seeking for most of his adult life.

Driving through the pouring rain, desperate to do something that would make things right, Hunter composed in his head the most apologetic, conciliatory, pleading e-mail he had ever written. Once home, he spent hour after hour — time that should have gone to detail-sanding wooden parts — perfecting the letter, scrutinizing every word. He sent it to the address he had from their previous correspondence as well as the new one he found on her website. He did not hear back for almost a week.

"I appreciate finally getting an explanation for why you ignored all my attempts to communicate with you. I suppose I should thank you. Your rudeness was the last straw, and since then I haven't been the least bit tempted to correspond with or get involved with anyone else. My condo is barely big enough for me, but I'm much happier living and teaching in Philadelphia than I was in Erie. Good luck in your search."

He tried again, this time listing all the advantages he felt he could offer her whether she moved to Toronto or he emigrated to Philadelphia.

She wrote back: "Since I am not rude enough to stop corresponding without notification, please understand that I have made it clear I don't wish any communication with you. Future e-mails you send me will get no response."

Pissed, he wrote back, "Fine, I'll build your damn time machine, then." He closed the laptop lid and looked around his converted kitchen/workshop. Brass bits, metal filings, worn pieces of sandpaper, oak scraps and several needle files covered the workbench. He had shipped out his latest finished piece that morning and had about six weeks to complete the next one, a relatively simple mangonel.

He ran his hand through his hair and pondered time travel paradoxes. The only way to definitely avoid encountering himself in the past would be to carry a time machine down to the States first. Of course, he could not imagine what it would take to get such a contraption over the border. How the hell big would it have to be, anyway? He supposed first he should worry about how in the world he could transport a human body, intact, backward through time.

But, maybe, he didn't really have to go back himself. Melinda had taken offense that he had stopped writing. He just needed to come up with a way to keep the correspondence going for the year between when he stopped writing and her trip to Toronto.

Hunter bartered with Derrick, giving him a

handful of 24-volt mercury relays, a bellows camera, and sharpening his chainsaw in exchange for his friend's older, still-working smart phone. Derrick had replaced it six months prior because he could never get reliable service where he lived or worked. But, he had paid the service charges on it for almost two years and it had always functioned properly at Hunter's house.

If Hunter could send the phone back in time, programmed to deliver an e-mail message to Melinda, he could pick up their correspondence where he'd left off. He just had to figure out how to open a wormhole into the past long enough to transport the smart phone through it.

After nearly three weeks of tinkering, dismayed by his lack of progress, he started work on the mangonel. While Hunter was searching for parts at the scrap yard, one of the drivers returned with a load scavenged from the university science department. Among warped steel shelving, copper shavings, and battered office furniture, Hunter found some extraordinary items, including the most powerful high-voltage supply he had ever seen at a scrap yard, a high-speed precision gyroscope, and a contraption so bizarre that it took him several minutes to even figure out it was a centrifuge.

He left without the pieces he needed for the mangonel, but he paid less than ten dollars for everything he had collected from the university's scrap. When he returned to his workshop, he realized the machine he had tried to create now required rebuilding to accommodate the new parts. Hunter worked through the night and most of the following day. He finally collapsed at four in the afternoon, too tired to even determine if his time machine functioned.

After sleeping almost ten hours, Hunter returned to the kitchen/workshop and scarfed down an oatmeal-apple muffin while he waited for his old laptop to wake up and the coffee to brew. Properly caffeinated, he fired up his new creation, which he had christened the Comuntimerator. Since he never intended anyone else to see this piece, he had forgone the usual time-consuming artistic touches that set his machines apart — no etched brass or carved and polished wood. It looked like something salvaged from a Jules Verne story.

He moved it to a corner of the shop where he tended to pile scrap he found less useful at home than it had seemed in the yard. After programming the smart phone, he set it in the Comuntimerator's cavity. When he flipped the switch, a blinding flash of light left him blinking and unsteady on his feet. The machine had emitted a crack so loud, the entire scrap pile shifted with several pieces bouncing off his boots. The stack of old issues of Physical Review, Compound Semiconductor, and Apeiron that he had meant to drop off at the local library for the past year toppled over and spilled out across the floor. He had to dig through the clutter to find the smart phone — a good sign, as it should have been laying about in his scrap heap for more than a year now.

Searching on his laptop through hundreds of e-mails in his inbox, he found the message he had typed into the smart phone before sending it back in time. It had a posting date of eleven months prior. He grinned, plugged the smart phone into its battery charger, and celebrated with another cup of coffee. Balancing his laptop in between the drill press and sander on an industrial-weight wheeled trolley he had scored from a salvage yard, he downloaded Melinda's last e-mail into the smart phone and hit reply. He apologized for not responding to the two previous emails she had sent, answering her phone calls, or acknowledging her IMs.

Using old e-mail to remind himself of his activities during the few weeks between his last missive to her and her final note, he constructed a plausible update. He set it to send from a dormant e-mail address that had been collecting spam for a couple of years, and concocted an explanation about why he stopped using his old one. He didn't need to stumble across her response when it originally arrived.

Immediately after he again dug the smart phone out of the scrap, he found her answer waiting in the inbox of the revived address. But he wanted to draw out his correspondence with Melinda, since the e-mail was just a delaying tactic, and he needed to finish the mangonel.

So Hunter did not read her response until several days later when the mangonel was packed and ready for posting.

When he opened her message, he almost choked on his lager. "Last week I received both an excellent offer on my house and an opportunity for a tenure-track position if I move to Philly. I'm afraid if you can't make it down for the laboratory analysis in the next week, I'll have to accept and move forward with my relocation plans. I can only afford a very small place in the city. I'd no longer have the room that I do now, for you or your workshop."

Hunter refrained from throwing the bottle across the room only because he did not want to clean up the mess. He rested his forehead on the cold steel of the workbench. Time to abandon ship, acknowledge that he had screwed up his one chance with her, and move on. But, he had sent the smart phone back through time twice. His machine worked. How much more complicated could it be to create a wormhole big enough to send himself into the past? He just had to scale up the machinery.

"Back to the scrap yards," he said to the computer.

After visiting every yard within a ten-kilometer radius of his north Toronto home, collecting various flotsam and jetsam he thought might someday prove useful, Hunter ventured across Lake Ontario to the Stoney Creek area. There he scored, big time. In the back of the lot, propped up against a pile of scrap aluminum extrusion, he found something that looked like a cross between a speedboat and a spaceship. Three meters long, by a meter and a half wide and meticulously crafted from half-centimeter brass, it had room in the bow for the various components he would need to power his machine and he would still be able to get himself inside.

By reminding the scale tender that the sale saved him the time and energy of chopping it up with a Sawzall, Hunter negotiated him down from three-fifty to two bones a kilo. The tender even helped load it onto the bed of Hunter's pickup truck.

When he returned home, Hunter realized he did not have room to work on the machine in his shop. He dragged the brass hull into the middle of his lounge, planting it between a bench covered with a wolverine pelt and a table he had built out of scrap wood a decade ago using a Swiss army knife and a rock.

Before he disassembled the Comuntimerator to scavenge the parts he would need, he optimistically composed an e-mail to Melinda on the smart phone with the logistics of his visit to Erie, Pennsylvania, a year ago June.

A month later, many of his tools had migrated from his normally organized workshop into the scattered fray of the lounge. The machine components were assembled and connected in the center of the bow at the far end from the opening in the back. This left room for his feet in the hollows that extended to diamond-shaped frames past where the bow narrowed to a point. His legs could slide in on either side of the machinery, which would extend up to his knees. He debated encasing the works in an aluminum housing. But his search of the interwebs for information on whether he had any hope of bringing what he now called his Transportimerator across the border, left him fairly sure he would not succeed. If he did not need to hide the machinery from curious border guards, he saw no reason to invest the extra time and material in concealing the inner workings.

When he decided the Transportimerator was complete, Hunter ran his hand over the polished surface and tried to figure out how in the world he could test it. He had created the Comuntimerator to open a wormhole and send an object through while the machine itself stayed in present time. But the Transportimerator was built to go through the wormhole with its passenger so he had designed it to travel forward in time as well as backwards. But, someone had to program the controls to reverse the machine's direction. Hunter saw no other option, but to try it out himself. He looked at the clock. In four hours, the pile driver that had roused him at seven in the morning the last three days should start back to work on the new building two doors down. Hunter decided to grab some sleep.

For once Hunter did not curse the unseen operator when the pounding woke him. Still half asleep, he brewed espresso powder in his percolator. Awake, but with his nerves on edge, he programmed the Transportimerator to send himself back four months to the third of May, when he would have been in California for the annual Maker Faire. He had to steady his hands against the cold brass before climbing inside. Hunter pulled the hatch to, took a deep breath, and flipped the switch.

The engine roared to life and its pitch increased to a whine. The metal hummed from vibrations that built to violent shaking. He clung to the two bicycle handles he had welded to either side, until his fingers hurt. When the engine finally cut out and the Transportimerator ceased its oscillations, Hunter took another deep breath. He slithered out of the machine and looked around. Amazingly, despite the noise, light, and vibrations, nothing in the lounge seemed out of place. Of course he did not know what it looked like four months from now when he left. Still, if he had destroyed his furniture, he should have remembered coming back to that after the Maker Faire.

Hunter wandered into his kitchen/work-shop. He noted the detritus of the piece that he had completed just in time to take it to the Faire scattered on the workbench. On the stove, the pan he had used to heat and thicken linseed oil stood next to a pot which still had marinara residue clinging to the sides. He had avoided heating linseed oil while cooking ever since, as the odor had permeated his sauce, making it barely edible. He touched the pot with one finger. "Cripes," he said aloud. Placing his hand against the side, he confirmed that the pot was still warm. Given its temperature, he must have arrived on Friday instead of Saturday, missing himself by less than an hour.

Hunter pulled out an unusual hexagonal red brass fitting he'd discovered at the scrap yard and buried it in one of the bins he had installed between his workbench and the wall. He climbed into the machine and set the controls to take him back to the day after he left the future in August. He would regret missing a full day of work time, but given the apparent variance, he did not know how else to avoid any possibility of encountering himself. He listened to the neighborhood before firing up the Transportimerator. The pile driver would not start work for several more months, but he could hear the wood chipper that had kept him from sleeping for the week before the Faire while a crew cleared trees from the lot where construction would soon begin. He hoped that would provide enough noise to cover the Transportimerator's return to present time.

When he emerged from the Transportimerator, Hunter discovered the tools scattered about his lounge had migrated toward the wall. The table and bench lay on their sides. Now, he did remember returning from the Maker Faire to find his lounge in disarray. At the time, he had suspected that his friend Ralph, who had the spare key, had spent the night because he was too intoxicated to drive back to Vaughan after a party.

According to the time on his cell phone, he had returned just three hours after he left, but Hunter felt as worn out as if he had rummaged around in scrap yards all day. He crawled back into bed, and even the pile driver could not keep him awake. When he regained consciousness around three, he dug out the hexagonal red brass fitting buried in the bin, just to assure himself he had succeeded. Then he pried open the casing of the Transportimerator's timing mechanism.

After several hours of fine tuning to improve the machine's precision, he made a few phone calls. Hunter persuaded Derrick to check on the place and retrieve the mail, in case his travels kept him away from home for any length of time. He expected to return within a day of when he left, but just to be safe, he set up automatic payments for rent and utilities for the next few months.

Without the option of taking the Transportimerator across the border, Hunter decided to haul it up to Ralph's property on the east end of Night Hawk Lake, an eight-hour-plus drive north of Toronto. There, he would not have to worry about whether construction crews would make enough ruckus to cover the noise of opening the wormhole or whether someone might stumble upon the Transportimerator while he ventured to the States. Since he had not visited the property in three years, he also had no concerns about encountering himself.

Ralph had purchased the property cheap when one of the mines in the area went under. Although he had intended to build a vacation cabin there, he had never done more than camp a few times on the three-acre, wooded lot. Ralph, who could be counted on to offer assistance without asking a lot of questions, helped Hunter load the Transportimerator onto the back of his truck.

Before he headed north, Hunter made sure he had all of Melinda's contact information as well as the address of the place where she had promised to meet him in downtown Erie near the bus station. He pulled as much cash as he dared out of his checking account. Fortunately, the mangonel buyer had appreciated the machine enough to add a bonus.

Hunter relaxed on the drive up to Night Hawk Lake. He rolled the truck windows down to enjoy the end-of-summer weather. Once he turned on PR 11 north of Huntsville, he encountered almost no traffic. Arriving at Ralph's property, Hunter parked the truck amidst the shrubbery closest to the lake where no one would be likely to spot it.

After dragging the Transportimerator out of the truck bed, Hunter covered the vehicle with a camouflage tarp as an additional precaution. He stuffed a second tarp and a backpack containing a couple of changes of clothes, the smart phone, some bottled water, and a few energy bars, into the hull of the Transportimerator. He took a deep breath and climbed inside, trying to ignore the queasy feeling in the pit of his stomach.

After checking and rechecking his settings, he flipped the switch. The whine did not seem as high pitched or the shaking as violent as it had the first time. Hunter supposed he could become as blasé about time travel as any other mode of transportation, if he did it often enough.

When the engine finally cut out and Hunter emerged from the Transportimerator, freezing rain had replaced the warm sunshine. He shivered and wished he had brought his parka instead of just a waterproof jacket, but he had not remembered such foul weather the previous June. He cursed himself for not checking, especially after the records set for rain just last month. Covering the Transportimerator with the tarp he'd brought along, Hunter slung the pack onto his back and hiked off toward PR 101 to hitch a ride into Matheson. He only saw five cars and no one stopped, so he had to walk almost fifteen kilometers in the icy downpour. When he arrived cold and drenched in the town of twenty-five hundred, he took refuge in the Northern Delight Restaurant. He asked the buxom blonde waitress what day it was, and watched her edge closer to the telephone on the wall behind the counter.

"I've been camping out in the woods and I lost track." He realized he did not have nearly enough gear for that. "My truck died and I had to hike out to see if I can find an alternator."

She laughed. "Only if you've got a few weeks to wait for it to get here." The tension in her shoulders eased. "It's the seventh of June. You wanna cup of coffee?"

"Sure. Still two thousand seven, right?" He laughed and sat at one of the bar stools in front of the lunch counter.

"Last time I checked." She plunked a stained ceramic cup down in front of him and filled it.

Hunter let out the breath he had not realized he was holding. He had succeeded in traveling back in time fourteen months. Inhaling the acrid aroma of coffee that had sat on the burner too long, he wrapped his hands around the cup to warm them. According to the clock, he had an hour and a half before the southbound coach would pass through town — this time the Transportimerator had been less than an hour off.

When the coach motored into downtown Toronto the next day, Hunter could finally get service on the smart phone. He called Melinda to confirm his departure from Canada and his expected arrival in Erie.

"Your visit gave me the incentive to get through the galleys." He loved the sound of her voice. "I just put them in the mail back to the publisher, so I won't be distracted by that while you're here."

"Excellent. I'm looking forward to finally meeting."

"Me, too. I need to start working on my marketing plan, but that can wait a few days."

"Will you be promoting the book in Canada?" Given the reaction he had witnessed at her Toronto appearance, Hunter knew her ideas about ways to adapt to the new economic reality appealed to his countrymen.

"No, mostly Ohio, Pennsylvania, Maryland, and New York. The publisher won't put a lot of resources into a book tour."

"You might want to investigate the Canadian market." He had to at least make sure she traveled to Toronto for their meeting at the convention center so she would inspire him to build the Transportimerator. "I think you'll get an enthusiastic response up here, perhaps even more positive than in the States."

"Thanks for the tip. I'll pass it along to my publisher. See you soon."

The trip to Erie proved uneventful. For once

even the border guards did not harass him. Of course, unlike his annual visits to the Maker Faire, he had no trebuchets, mangonels, or ballistas with his gear. When the bus finally pulled into the Greyhound station on Peach Street in Erie, Hunter was a bit unsteady walking across the street to the gigantic shopping mall. He attributed his wooziness to the fact that he had spent more than fifteen of the past twenty-four hours riding the coaches. He stopped in the men's room to freshen up before entering the restaurant and realized his hands were shaking. After devoting the last several months of his life, as well as considerable funds, to travel back in time so he could rectify a mistake he made a year and a half ago, he had to ask himself if the possibility of hooking up with anyone could really merit that much effort.

Leaning on the basin, he stared at himself in the mirror. His beard definitely had more grey streaks than he remembered, and he could see additional wrinkles surrounding his eyes. "Sure hope she's worth it," he muttered. Hunter pulled open the door and made his way into the restaurant to look for Melinda.

He found her at a table, typing into a notebook computer, looking even prettier than he remembered. In this light, her dark hair had auburn highlights. She wore a tailored white blouse that emphasized her beautiful breasts.

"Hey, there, how was your trip?" She offered him her hand.

Instead of shaking it, Hunter turned it and brought it to his lips. She gave him a smile that lit up her whole face and he could see green specks in the dark brown of her eyes. He felt swoony and had to sit down quickly.

She closed the lid of the notebook, without, he noticed, turning it off. "I wasn't sure if the bus would get here on time, so I figured I'd catch up on some e-mail."

Although he had subsisted mostly on energy bars with one greasy burger grabbed when the coach stopped to refuel, Hunter found nothing on the menu he thought could make it past a stomach that had suddenly gotten queasy again. He attributed it to nervousness and ordered a cola. "The picture you sent me doesn't do you justice."

She lowered her eyes and he wanted to kiss her. "Thanks. Cameras have never been kind to me."

Hunter reached across the table and took one of her hands in both of his. "I don't know about you, but my chemistry's working overtime."

Melinda looked up and her eyes shimmered. "Yeah, me too. I can't believe I finally met someone online — I swear, I've corresponded with more than a hundred guys. I'd pretty much given up on finding anyone. That's one of the reasons I put my house on the market. Then you sent me that first note."

Hunter ran his thumb back and forth across

her fingers. "Not the best time to be selling."

"I know, that's why I didn't want to pass on this offer."

"And now?"

The waitress returned, depositing Hunter's cola and Melinda's iced tea.

Melinda shrugged. "That depends. You willing to move to the States?"

"I'd have to give up a lot, even though I do live in a dump that's scheduled for demolition." Of course the sagging real estate market had indefinitely postponed razing the rest of the homes in his neighborhood, but the previous June he had not known that. Still, he could not imagine anyone as refined as Melinda living there.

"I know there's a lot of advantages in Canada, especially given the current administration here. But if I keep my place, there's room for you and your workshop."

Her smile made his stomach roil and he released her hand so he could take a long swig of his cola.

"My mortgage payments are small and after six months, if we file a domestic partnership, I can get you on my health plan at the college. Not exactly free medical care, but better than what most Americans have access to."

Hunter's vision got blurry and the room seemed to spin. He could not think and just muttered the first thing that came to mind. "Moving across the border is problematic at best. My shop is in Canada, my components, my connections for parts are all there. The logistics of relocating a working shop are formidable." He silently berated himself for throwing up roadblocks, although it did give him a moment to clear his head.

"I know. But if they're going to raze your building, you're going to have to move anyway."

"What if you took the offer on the house and we looked for a place in Toronto together?" He swallowed the rest of his cola and the room stopped spinning for a moment.

"Now's not exactly the best time to go job hunting either, especially for an American in Canada. I'd have to get a green card or whatever the Canadian equivalent is. At least, working for yourself, you could avoid some of the paperwork, especially if you continued selling through Canada."

"But what about the book, couldn't you make a living as a writer?"

She laughed. "I got a whole five grand advance, and I won't see any royalties for at least a year after it comes out which is next June. And this is kind of a one-time opportunistic project, I never saw it as anything I could turn into a livelihood. Given that it's aimed at consumers rather than economists, it probably won't even help me get tenure."

For the first time since he sat down, Hunter's stomach felt almost normal. He flagged the waitress down to ask for a refill.

The notebook pinged. "Excuse me for a second." Melinda lifted the lid. "My publisher said he'd get back to me quickly about pursuing the Canadian market." She tapped a couple of keys and looked up with a broad grin. "Apparently he did some research that corroborates your suspicions. He's decided to send me on a tour across the eastern provinces. Looks like I'll be in Toronto beginning of July next year."

Perfect timing, Hunter thought.

Her eyes sparkled, her smile reached out to caress him. "Of course, by then, hopefully, you will have moved down here."

The room swirled and Hunter's vision blurred. It did not matter when Melinda traveled to Toronto. Any visit, now, would be a planned reunion not a confrontation. He could not catch his breath. The table slammed into his face and cola spilled into his nose.

Hunter glanced at the clock, dismayed when he realized he had spent the past six hours buffing the housing of one marine lamp. He cursed the unusual dearth of quality artifacts at scrap yards in the area. Although he should have left for the convention center twenty minutes ago, he needed to spiff up first before he headed downtown. Abandoning the components scattered across the top of his primary workbench — a door harvested from a thrift shop dumpster then sheathed in sheet steel — he headed upstairs.

By the time Hunter showered, trimmed his mostly black goatee, combed his thinning black hair, removed the brass polish from under his fingernails, and put on clean clothing, he knew he would not make the lecture of the American he had "met" on a dating site. He arrived at the conference center just as Dr. Melinda Jacobson received an enthusiastic round of applause from the audience of about seventy-five. Hunter waited until the last autograph seeker finally left before approaching the beautiful brunette, who sat behind stacks of books at a table next to the podium.